Here comes Theo

For Anna

Library of Congress Catalog Card No. 88–80590

ISBN 0–316–32307–1
10   9   8   7   6   5   4   3   2   1

First published in Great Britain in 1984
by Hamish Hamilton Children's Books

Printed in Hong Kong by
South China Printing Co.

Here comes Theo

Bob Graham

Little, Brown and Company
Boston   Toronto

Theo sees something.
What can it be?

Look at his ears
and look at his tail.

Here comes Theo.

Look at him go.

Theo sees Sarah.
Look at him fly.

Watch out, Sarah!

Down she goes

and gets the licking treatment.

Next day Sarah is ready.

She catches Theo,

but he climbs right over her.

Down they go,

almost on top of John.

"Be CAREFUL, Theodore."

Sarah calls him Theodore
when she is angry.

John doesn't call him anything.

John can't talk properly yet.

He can't even walk.

Well, not quite.

He hauls himself up
on his rubbery legs . . .

But look, what's this?

He's taking a step!

Look at Theo's tail.

Look at John wobbling.

Here comes Theo.

He flies . . .

"THEODORE!"

Down goes John with a smack,

and gets the licking treatment.